PRAISE FOR

Basil of Baker Street

"First-rate detective fare."
—*Cleveland Press*

READ MORE ABOUT
Basil's adventures!

Basil and the Cave of Cats

COMING SOON

Basil in Mexico

THE
GREAT MOUSE DETECTIVE

Basil of Baker Street

BY *Eve Titus*

ILLUSTRATED BY *Paul Galdone*

ALADDIN

NEW YORK LONDON TORONTO SYDNEY NEW DELHI

ALADDIN

An imprint of Simon & Schuster Children's Publishing Division
1230 Avenue of the Americas, New York, New York 10020
This Aladdin paperback edition May 2016
Text copyright © 1958 by Eve Titus; copyright renewed © 1986 by Eve Titus
Interior illustrations copyright © 1958 by Paul Galdone; copyright renewed © 1986 by Paul Galdone
Cover illustration copyright © 2016 by David Mottram
Also available in an Aladdin hardcover edition.
All rights reserved, including the right of reproduction in whole or in part in any form.
ALADDIN is a trademark of Simon & Schuster, Inc., and related logo
is a registered trademark of Simon & Schuster, Inc.
For information about special discounts for bulk purchases, please contact
Simon & Schuster Special Sales at 1-866-506-1949 or business@simonandschuster.com.
The Simon & Schuster Speakers Bureau can bring authors to your live event.
For more information or to book an event contact the Simon & Schuster
Speakers Bureau at 1-866-248-3049 or visit our website at www.simonspeakers.com.
Cover designed by Karin Paprocki
Interior designed by Mike Rosamilia
The text of this book was set in Perpetua.
Manufactured in the United States of America 0416 OFF
2 4 6 8 10 9 7 5 3 1
Library of Congress Control Number 2015955960
ISBN 978-1-4814-6402-4 (hc)
ISBN 978-1-4814-6401-7 (pbk)
ISBN 978-1-4814-6403-1 (eBook)

To Adrian M. Conan Doyle
in the humble hope
that this book for boys and girls
will be a bridge
to Mr. Sherlock Holmes himself

Cast of Characters

BASIL   *an English mouse detective*

DR. DAWSON   *his friend and associate*

ANGELA AND AGATHA   *the mouse twins who vanish*

MR. AND MRS. PROUDFOOT   *their loving parents*

MRS. JUDSON   *a mousekeeper*

SAM STILTON   *a talkative mouse shopkeeper*

A MYSTERIOUS MESSENGER

POLICE CONSTABLE CLEWES

THE TERRIBLE THREE

SAILORS

POLICE

Contents

1

BASIL, THE
SUPER SLEUTH

THE MYSTERY OF THE MISSING TWINS COULD never have been solved by an ordinary detective.

But Basil, of course, was far from ordinary. Even before the kidnappers' note came, his keen mind had deduced what the criminals really wanted.

"Mark my words," he told me, "the disappearance of Angela and Agatha is only the beginning. The criminals plan to strike at all of us!"

He was quite right. But there was a long and dangerous road to be traveled before the pieces of the puzzle fell into place.

Who masterminded the plot? What was the motive behind it? How were the twins lured away?

And Basil—what sort of sleuth was he?

To make these matters clear, I shall tell you something of his amazing career as a detective, and then relate the events leading up to the crime.

The place is London, in the year 1885. . . .

Pray allow me to introduce myself. I am Dr. David Q. Dawson, Basil's close friend and associate.

Basil was as famous a detective in our world as was Mr. Sherlock Holmes in the world of people.

This came about because he studied at the feet of Mr. Holmes himself, visiting him regularly in his rooms at Baker Street, Number 221B.

I usually went along. We would scurry up to the sitting room shared by Sherlock and Dr. John H. Watson. Well-hidden, we would then listen closely as Mr. Holmes told his friend exactly how he solved his cases.

Thus Basil learned the scientific side of sleuthing from the best teacher of them all.

Mr. Holmes was tall and thin, with sharp, piercing eyes. And if ever a mouse may be said to resemble a man, then Basil was the mouse!

He even dressed like his hero, thanks to a clever little tailor who copied Sherlock's wardrobe almost exactly.

But the long trips to Baker Street, in all sorts of weather, were tiring and often risky. We braved many a blizzard to reach our goal.

One evening, leaving by way of the cellar, Basil stopped so suddenly that I almost bumped into him.

"Observe, my dear doctor," he remarked,

pointing with his walking stick. "Observe how clean and spacious is this cellar. What a far cry from our crowded, dingy dwellings in the East End!"

His eyes lit up. "We could build a town here. Picture a row of cozy flats on that empty shelf next to the front windows—plus shops, a school, a library, a town hall, and other buildings. A name for the town? Ah, I have it—Holmestead!"

"A brilliant idea, Basil! Best of all, we could steal upstairs to listen to our beloved Sherlock as often as we pleased."

"Precisely," said my companion, smiling. "We shall put it to a vote at our next town hall meeting."

The forty-four families in our community approved.

Basil drew up the plans. Carpenters traveled to Baker Street night after night, working at breakneck speed, and within two weeks the move was made.

Holmestead was a model town, and mice from all over London came to look and to marvel.

The flat Basil and I shared fronted the street, so that we could see our callers before they entered, just as Mr. Holmes did.

Basil listened long and often to the master, and it soon seemed as though there were no mystery too tangled for him to unravel.

Mice journeyed long distances to consult him, even French mice from across the Channel. Rich or poor, no one in need of help was ever turned from his door.

He brought so many criminals to justice that evildoers trembled at the mere mention of his name.

Then, but one month after we had moved to Baker Street, the strangest case of Basil's career began.

Angela and Agatha, our neighbors' young twins, vanished into thin air!

2

WHERE ARE
THE TWINS?

WHEN THE TWINS' PARENTS CAME TO OUR ROOMS
late at night, seeking Basil's help, we were upstairs.

Unnoticed, we sat in our favorite corner, listening with deep interest.

Mr. Holmes was telling Dr. Watson in detail
exactly how he had solved a jewel burglary that
had completely baffled Scotland Yard.

Basil whipped out his notebook and jotted
down every word, scribbling rapidly in shorthand, or perhaps I should say shortpaw.

"What sheer genius!" he whispered. "What a
brain! That man will become a legend—his fame
has spread to the far corners of the earth."

"You are something of a legend yourself," said I.

"Perhaps, Dawson, but I still have much to learn. What an honor it is to study under Sherlock Holmes!"

To which I answered, "And what an honor for *me* to be associated with the Sherlock Holmes of the Mouse World!"

Basil bowed modestly and resumed taking notes.

About an hour or so later, Mr. Holmes took his violin from its case. He put a new E string on the instrument, discarding the old one in the wastebasket.

Then he lifted his bow and dashed off a piece by Paganini. We were all ears, for he played it magnificently.

"Bravo!" squeaked Basil, quite carried away.

Next, we heard a Mendelssohn piece, requested by Dr. Watson, after which the two men retired to their bedrooms.

Basil took the E string from the basket, and we scurried silently across the floor to our secret passageway.

I should mention here that my friend had made one very strict rule when we moved to Baker Street.

The rule was laid down because he did not wish to risk disturbing his hero in any way whatsoever.

It stated that only Basil and myself were allowed upstairs—no other mouse was even to venture near our passageway. It was therefore with great surprise that we saw someone hurrying to meet us. It was Mrs. Judson, our mousekeeper.

She was considerably upset. "Oh, Mr. Basil," she wailed, "I know I'm breaking the rule, but this is an emergency! The Proudfoots, your neighbors, have been waiting in your rooms for an hour. And

Mrs. Proudfoot hasn't stopped crying since the moment she came. I just *had* to fetch you!"

"Pray calm yourself, and tell us what has occurred," said Basil kindly.

"Angela and Agatha have disappeared!"

"That's odd," I remarked. "However, the twins are known to be mischievous. No doubt it is a childish prank of some sort."

"I hardly think so," said Basil. "The hour is far too late for that. It bears looking into—let's hurry our steps a bit."

Mrs. Judson's apron strings bobbed back and forth as she ran on ahead, and in a matter of minutes we reached our rooms.

I was shocked by the change in Mrs. Proudfoot. She was an attractive white mouse, who usually looked gay and youthful. Now her red-rimmed eyes and tear-swollen face made her seem years older.

As Basil strode into the sitting room, she sprang from her chair and clutched at his lapels.

"Our twins are missing! They vanished on the way home from school. What dreadful thing could have happened to them? A mousetrap, perhaps? Oh, my poor dears—where can they be?"

She sank back on the sofa, sobbing. I took a bottle of smelling salts from my little black bag, and waved it under her nose.

The father stood silently by, with a look of extreme suffering on his face.

Basil opened his notebook. "Your wife is much too upset to talk. Will you tell me all you know?"

Mr. Proudfoot braced himself. "I shall try, sir. Angela and Agatha never return home from school later than four o'clock. Now it is past eleven at night, and we are at our wits' end! You know the twins—they are happy, contented children, and contented children do not run away from home."

"You are right on that point, Mr. Proudfoot. Have you questioned their schoolmates?"

"Yes. They said the twins had planned to stop at the sweetshop on their way home from school. They do this often, for they have an especial fondness for chocolates. That's where most of their allowance goes. But when we spoke to the sweetshop proprietor, he said they hadn't arrived there this afternoon."

"Do you trust the proprietor?" asked Basil.

"Mr. Hume is one of the most honest mice I know."

"H'm. Then we can eliminate him as a suspect. One last question—what were the twins wearing?"

"You'll have to ask my wife that."

"Pretty pink pinafores," said Mrs. Proudfoot tearfully. "My precious darlings always looked so sweet in pink, with their little white faces—"

Basil patted her shoulder. "I can offer you only crumbs of comfort now. But rest assured that I shall do all in my power to restore your twins to you.

For your own sake, go home and try to get some sleep."

She leaned heavily on her husband as they walked to the door. Mr. Proudfoot turned around.

"You are the only one who can help us. You *will* find them, won't you?"

"My investigations begin at once," replied the detective. "I hope to have news soon—good news."

As soon as they had gone, he said, "My first step in the Mystery of the Missing Twins will be to hunt for clues. Come along, my dear doctor, and bring a candlestick—we're off to the sweetshop!"

3

THE TELLTALE
FOOTPRINTS

IT WAS WELL PAST MIDNIGHT. A TINY NIGHT LIGHT
glowed in the windows of the closed shop, the
last in the row. Holmestead ended there. Beyond
lay the blackness of the cellar, vast and menacing.

Basil paced back and forth, pondering the
problem.

"If I remember rightly, there should be an
emergency exit ten yards ahead."

"There is, Basil. But it is in the darkest part of
the cellar, and no one ever goes there."

He gripped my arm. "Then we shall be the first!
There may be clues. Light the candle, Dawson."

I did as he asked. He took out his pocket

magnifying glass and peered through it, stooping low as he moved slowly toward the door. Not one inch of ground escaped his sharp eyes.

I was surprised to find that the emergency door was wide open.

Basil studied the pavement. "Ah! The dust here has been recently disturbed."

Flinging himself full length upon the ground, he used his lens both inside and outside the door.

"Dawson, this dust has a story to tell. There are three sets of big footprints, and two sets of little ones. The owner of one big set went inside, as far as the sweetshop, while his friends waited outside. There are no signs of a struggle here. The small footprints followed the big ones willingly!"

His face was stern as he rose to his full height.

"The twins have always been warned not to talk to strangers. Picture the pair on their way to the sweetshop, sad because it is near the end of the week and their allowance is almost gone. Just beyond the shop stands a smiling stranger, in whose outstretched paws they see something most tempting—French chocolates! He beckons and they follow, completely forgetting their parents' warnings!"

He closed the door. "There is nothing more we can learn here."

Back in our rooms, Basil filled his berrywood pipe and curled up in an easy chair, deep in thought.

I skimmed the pages of the *London Mouse Daily*.

At last Basil spoke. "A sinister plot has been hatched by a daring band of criminals. It cannot be money they want, for the Proudfoots have scarcely a crumb to their name!

"Mark my words, Dawson—this gang is after something more important to them than money. What it may be, we have yet to learn. Kidnappers usually send a note. I expect they will get in touch with us soon, possibly tomorrow."

Unwinding his long legs, he strode over to the wooden mantelpiece, where he stood staring at his treasured collection of Holmes souvenirs.

There were scraps of paper his hero had written upon, old pen points he had used, a torn blotter, a broken pocket lens, a whittling of Holmes done by Basil himself, and other odds and ends.

"No doubt the master would have solved this case by now," said my companion glumly.

"Not even *he* could have done more than you have, Basil, with so few clues."

"Perhaps, perhaps," he muttered impatiently.

"But how maddening it is to sit and wait! Think of those poor children, heaven knows where—"

The detective's face darkened, and his eyes flashed fire.

"Dawson, the most contemptible creatures on the face of this earth are kidnappers! They are indeed the lowest of the low!"

4

A DAY OF
SUSPENSE

ALL THE NEXT MORNING BASIL LOUNGED ABOUT
in his Persian robe, his mood one of blackest gloom.

Mr. Proudfoot called upon us. Basil told him
he was awaiting word from those responsible for
the twins' disappearance.

"Then it's as I feared," said the father grimly.
"Angela and Agatha have been kidnapped!"

"That is what the clues indicate," the detective
admitted. "However, I promised to bring them
back unharmed, and I shall."

Mr. Proudfoot brightened. "I'll repeat your
words to my wife. We have the utmost faith in you."

After lunch, Basil took out the block of wood

he was whittling into a violin. He had been working on it for some weeks.

As he whittled I could tell that his keen brain was busy with the clues he had thus far uncovered.

At one point he announced, "I believe I have deduced what the criminals want. If I am right, our town's entire future is in peril! Ask me nothing now. I shall learn whether my suspicions are correct when the kidnappers' note arrives."

I had a hundred questions, but kept silent, continuing to read *Mouse About Town,* a library book.

From time to time the doorbell rang. Mrs. Judson answered, and I could hear children inquiring after the twins. She said sadly that there was no news.

The day dragged on. Late in the afternoon, Basil held up the finished violin, a fine piece of work.

He snipped off part of the E string taken from Mr. Holmes' basket, and put it on his own instrument.

"Now that I have all four strings, I, too, shall make music. I studied the violin many years ago and must surely remember a little of what I learned."

"I hope so, Basil. Nothing pains me more than badly played music!"

He bowed his head. "I shall do my best."

But alas, he attempted the difficult Paganini piece Mr. Holmes had played the night before. Terribly out of practice, he struck so many wrong notes that I put my paws to my ears!

"In heaven's name, stop! For my sake and for poor Paganini's too—we are suffering!"

He twanged one of the strings.

"My dear doctor, be comforted by the thought that these strings are made of catgut!"

Chuckling, I rang for Mrs. Judson, who soon bustled in with our tea.

Holding my cup, I strolled over to the window.

Baker Street was covered with ice. Walking was unsafe, and the street was practically deserted.

Suddenly I saw a plump, middle-aged mouse slipping and sliding along, squinting up at the house numbers.

"Basil, there's a strange mouse outside."

He rushed over and drew aside the lace curtain.

"Aha! Our long wait is over. Unless I am much mistaken, this is the messenger from the kidnappers!"

5

THE MYSTERIOUS
MESSENGER

THE LOUD CLANGING OF THE BELL WAS WELCOME music to our ears, and we hastened to answer it ourselves.

Upon the doorstep stood the tubby mouse. His corduroy jacket was old and baggy, and its collar was turned up against the cold.

He removed his shabby cloth cap and began to twirl it nervously, shuffling his feet back and forth.

"Beggin' your pardon, sirs, but which one o' you is Mr. Basil, the detective?"

"I am he. Pray state your business."

The messenger reached in his pocket. Out came an old toy kitten minus its tail. He crammed this back into his pocket and then drew out a blue envelope.

"I was told to give you this, Mr. Basil."

"And by whom, may I inquire?"

Cold as it was, beads of sweat stood out on the messenger's brow.

In great terror he said, "Please, sir, don't be askin' me that. I swore I wouldn't tell! Good day."

And the plump mouse ran down Baker Street as though he were being chased by a thousand tomcats!

We stared after him. "What a pity that we learned nothing at all about him," I remarked. "It might have been of help in solving this case."

"That's where you are wrong," replied Basil. "I already know a great deal about our mysterious messenger. What did you yourself gather?"

"Nothing much, except that he's poor and that he's a family mouse—the toy kitten, you know."

"True enough," agreed my friend. "But those facts are obvious. You are not making full use of your deductive powers."

"Tell me, then," said I, somewhat annoyed at his tone, "what did *you* deduce?"

"He was once a sailor, he now follows the trade of carpenter, and he comes from the Northwest of England. Near the coast, I'd say. Furthermore, his initials are H. H., and he traveled here by train."

I was astounded. "But how on earth do you know all that?"

"It is really quite simple. The clues are always at hand, if one's mind is trained to observe them.

"I immediately perceived the tiny mermaid tattooed on his wrist. And it is a proven fact that most sailors who take to land settle as near to the sea as they can get. As for his trade, did you not notice the outlines of the carpenter's rule in his pocket? His speech betrayed his nesting place—I could not mistake those Northwest accents. His initials were in the lining of the cap he kept twirling, and he had succeeded in brushing off some of the train soot, but not quite all of it."

"Basil, you are a magician!"

"Furthermore, his marriage is most happy."

"Now you are jesting," I said. "There was no way for you to deduce that fact."

Basil's brows shot upward. "Wasn't there? I noticed a large patch on his sleeve. It was not the work of a skilled tailor, but it was lovingly and carefully sewn. Only a devoted relative would have gone to such pains. I am sure it is his wife, for the toy kitten tells us he is a father."

"Amazing!" I exclaimed.

"Elementary, my dear Dawson."

We went inside and seated ourselves on either side of the flickering fire.

The blaze crackled cheerily, and the dancing flames seemed like little rays of hope. I brightened at the thought that the kidnappers might have written to say that the twins were on their way home at that very moment.

Basil unsealed the envelope and carefully removed the typewritten note inside.

Without turning a whisker, he read it aloud, slowly. I marveled at his complete calm. As for myself, cold chills ran up and down my spine!

6

THE KIDNAPPERS' NOTE

BAKER STREET MICE—B E W A R E !

So far the twins are safe. They'll stay that
way if you do what we say. We've decided to
make your Baker Street cellar the headquarters
for our gang. Everybody must get out in 48
hours. It's Basil's job to move you all out, just
the way he moved you in. Better make it fast!
And leave the furniture—we need it.

This is the only warning you'll get. And listen—
if you don't follow our orders, you'll never set
eyes on those twins again!

THE TERRIBLE THREE

"Great heavens," I cried, "what a horrible affair! It's enough to make one's fur stand on end! Are we to be driven from our homes by these scoundrels? Can nothing be done to stop them? And yet we must think of Angela and Agatha—"

Basil's lean jaw tightened. "The cunning devils! Here at Baker Street, the Terrible Three would be in the heart of London, within easy reach of all its riches! Protected by bodyguards, they could sit in this very cellar and organize the gangs already in this great city. They could plan their crimes for them and make a mockery of law and order!"

I nodded. "No honest mouse would be safe— they would rule us all! Do you think the messenger is one of the Terrible Three?"

"No. His guilty manner showed he knew the contents of the note, but he is too new at this game. He is our one lead—only through him can we hope to reach the criminals."

"Then they are using him as a cat's-paw," I said, "by threats against his family. That mouse was haunted by fear! Remember how nervously he kept shuffling his feet?"

Basil leaped excitedly from his chair. "By Jove,

Dawson, I've been a fool! I've overlooked a most important clue!"

He snatched a sheet of paper from the desk and dashed outside. I followed close on his heels.

"Mrs. Judson hasn't swept off the doorstep—thank heaven for that!"

He got on his knees and scraped at some dried earth with his penknife. Then he scooped it up on the paper and carried it carefully inside.

Placing the earth on a glass slide, he examined it under a low-power microscope. When he straightened up, there was a smile of triumph on his face.

He motioned me toward the microscope. "Tell me what you see, Dawson."

I bent over and looked through the lens. "Earth."

"Ah, but what kind of earth?"

"I don't know. There's some darker substance mixed in with it—can it be coal dust?"

"Precisely. The traces of coal dust will tell us where our carpenter lives. And you may be sure the Terrible Three will be nearby."

He looked thoughtful. "H'm. There are three coastal towns in the Northwest of England where the coal mines extend beneath the bed of the

ocean—Whitehaven, Workington, and Maryport.
These are people's towns, of course. Kindly hand
me the *Mouse's Atlas.*"

He scanned several maps. "Aha! One mile
south of Workington is the town of Mousecliffe-
on-Sea. It has a fine harbor. Population—958 in
winter, double that in summer. Now we know
where our carpenter lives."

He snapped the heavy volume shut. "No one,
not even the Proudfoots, must know of the note.
All of Holmestead would be in a panic! I believe

31

I can capture the villains before the forty-eight hours are up. But no time must be lost!"

He vanished into the next room. Ten minutes later he emerged.

I sat there, utterly dumbfounded, unable to believe my eyes! And yet I should have been prepared, for Basil was a past master of the art of disguise. He not only knew makeup thoroughly but paid close attention to every detail of costume.

Often, on other cases, we had worn getups that would have fooled our own mothers.

This time I was astonished all over again. Had I not known it was Basil, I would have sworn it was some other mouse.

Gone was the stern, eagle-eyed detective!

In his place stood a weatherbeaten old sea captain with a droll, wrinkled face.

"Ahoy there, Matey!" Eyes twinkling, he did a few steps of a sailor's hornpipe.

Then he flung some sailor clothes at me. "Get into these, and I'll use greasepaint to turn our dignified doctor into a swaggering sea-mouse!"

He worked on my face. A bit later, I looked into the mirror—a cocky first mate with a black patch over one eye stared back.

I started to do the hornpipe, but Basil did not join me.

He was hunting impatiently through the mess of papers on his desk. At last he found what he wanted—a railroad timetable.

He pulled out his pocket watch. "A train leaves for Workington within the hour, from Euston Station. Let us each pack a few necessities. Then we'll be off, my nautical ne'er-do-well!"

I saluted smartly. "Aye, aye, Cap'n!"

7

WE TRAVEL
IN DISGUISE

OUTSIDE, THE FOG WAS AS THICK AS PEA SOUP, and we could barely see in front of our faces. Icy, slippery streets forced us to walk at a snail's pace.

"We'll never make the train at this rate," said I.

Basil pointed to a black hansom cab standing in front of a house. "Perhaps we can shorten our journey—let us wait and see."

We leaned against the iron railing, huddled together. The cold seemed to creep into our very bones.

Presently a gentleman emerged. We heard him tell the cabbie to drive to Euston Station.

"Luck is with us!" whispered my companion,

as we climbed up on the rear of the cab. "This will mean the saving of much valuable time."

The horse clop-clopped along. It was all we could do to hang on, for we were jounced and jolted about.

Euston Station was crowded with hurrying humans, whose feet we took care to avoid. Our small size served us well. Not a soul noticed us as we made our way to the platform and slipped into an empty first-class compartment.

The whistle blew and the train started, picking up speed until it fairly flew through the countryside.

Warm and snug in a corner of our compartment, we were glad of the chance to rest.

Basil stretched out his long legs and pulled his cap over his eyes, as was his habit when thinking deeply.

My own thoughts were far from happy. Every click of the wheels, speeding over the shining rails, brought us closer to the unknown perils that lay ahead.

Basil was sure he would solve this case before the forty-eight hours were up. His failures had been few, but what if this proved to be one of them?

He seemed to have read my mind, for he said, "'Pon my word, Dawson, you look as though the world were coming to an end! Surely you do not doubt that I shall solve this mystery? Never fear— I shall! Meanwhile, I'll teach you some sailors' lingo I picked up during my waterfront jaunts, for we must not betray our true identities to the Terrible Three or anyone else in Mousecliffe."

The phrases he taught me were fairly simple, and I practiced sailor talk for the rest of the trip.

At Workington, we found that the fog had lifted. A yellow moon cast an eerie glow over

Basil's face as he studied his pocket compass to determine our direction.

Our path lay along a narrow road that mounted a steep cliff. The ocean roared angrily, far below. The road descended into a valley, then continued through some thick woods.

Occasionally we heard an owl hooting. I quaked in my boots, having no wish to end my days as a juicy morsel for one of our age-old enemies. Fortunately, we met none of them face to face.

Dawn was breaking when at last we reached the

Greymouse Inn. A night clerk dozed in an easy chair. I nudged him gently. Yawning, he went behind the desk and pushed the guest book toward us.

Basil signed first, chuckling as he did so.

When my turn came, I saw that he had registered as Captain Baker, of Blackpool.

Not to be outdone, I signed myself Mr. Street, of Southampton.

Our room was large and airy. The sun was rising to signal the start of a new day, but every bone in my body cried out for a rest.

I lowered the blinds. "Captain Baker, your investigations must wait. We didn't sleep a wink last night."

"But, Mr. Street, I am fully awake, and plan to nose about down in the lobby. The town gossips might have some interesting information. May I expect the pleasure of my first mate's company?"

"You may not," I replied drowsily.

Fully clothed, I flung my tired body across one of the beds. My eyelids grew heavy, and I drifted into a deep, dreamless sleep.

8

BASIL MAKES
SOME DEDUCTIONS

"ARISE, MY SLUMBERING SEA-MOUSE! THE HOUR is noon."

I stirred, and stretched lazily. Bright sunlight shone full in my eyes.

Basil stood at my bedside, looking highly pleased with himself. "I had quite a chat with the innkeeper and am in possession of some helpful facts. Would you care to hear about it?"

"By all means," said I, propping myself up against my pillow.

"At first the innkeeper told me very little. Since he is a stay-at-home type, who has probably never been out of Mousecliffe, I deduced that he must depend upon the exploits of others for excitement. I won his good will with my imaginary adventures as captain of the stout ship *Pied Piper*. It would have warmed your heart to listen, for my first mate, Mr. Street, was always the hero!"

"Indeed!"

"When we fought unfriendly natives on a South Sea isle, *your* bravery, Mr. Street, saved the day. And in New York City, you rescued me from a tribe of wild bandits at the risk of your life!"

"Hear, hear," I cried, trying not to smile.

"In return for these tall tales, the innkeeper chatted about many Mousecliffe inhabitants. At last he got around to carpenters."

He rubbed his paws together in satisfaction.

"Our messenger's name is Harry Hawkins. He is well liked, and known as a fine carpenter. However, jobs have been scarce this past year. At times, his wife and their eight young ones almost starved. Then Hawkins' luck changed. He was hired to do some cabinetwork on the yacht *Victoria,* anchored here in the harbor, at a high rate of pay."

Basil smiled so broadly that I sat up in bed and said, "If you will pardon my mentioning the unmentionable, you look as smug as the cat that swallowed the canary. Can it be that the yacht has not one owner, but *three*?"

"Excellent! You are really learning to deduce, Dawson. No one knows them as the Terrible Three, of course, but I hear they are nasty characters, disliked for their overbearing ways."

I swung my feet to the floor. "This is all very interesting, Basil, but I happen to be hungry."

"Good. We lunch at the Flying Squirrel, down at the docks. The Terrible Three eat there quite often, and I'd like a look at the scoundrels. Afterward, we shall pay a few calls."

We freshened up a bit, and Basil applied touches of greasepaint where needed.

Then we sauntered out into the sunshine. It was a crisp, midwinter day, the sky was a beautiful blue, and Mousecliffe-on-Sea was a pretty town.

Our city-bred noses sniffed at the salty sea air and found it much to our liking. Since there were many sailors about, we attracted no attention.

At the Flying Squirrel we ordered cheese and chips. Just as our food arrived, we noticed three mice standing in the doorway.

I must say that I shouldn't have enjoyed encountering any of them alone in a dark alley!

They were more like apes than like mice, with their hulking shoulders and long, loose-hanging arms. They swaggered in, sneering at everyone they passed.

Basil, without seeming to do so, sharply scrutinized their faces.

One of them purposely pushed against our table. The plates almost slid off, and he laughed out loud.

Angry, I rose to my feet, but Basil whispered, "This is not the time," and I sat down meekly.

The Terrible Three were two tables away. Snatches of their talk came to our ears.

One of them said, "Let's eat here tonight. The food's a sight better than the slop we get aboard the yacht. The quicker we get hold of another ship's cook the better it'll be for our insides!"

He called over to Basil, "Cap'n, d'you know of a good ship's cook? We're willin' to pay well."

Basil shook his head. "Sorry, Matey. Our own cook aboard the *Pied Piper* is none too good. I'm in the same fix you are."

We paid our bill and left.

Rambling through town, he said, "I recognized them. Each is an expert in his own field of crime and has been behind bars. Now that I know where they will be early this evening, I have decided upon my course of action. They will find that they are not the only ones who can mastermind a plot!"

He halted in front of a grocer's shop. The sign above read: SAM STILTON, PROPRIETOR.

"Next we pay a call here. These places are usually gold mines of information, although I rather fancy I'll have to do a lot of listening before I find out what I wish to know. Pray do not be surprised if I sound like a gossip myself—it's give and take, you know."

He held the door open with a flourish and bowed low. "You first, my dear *first* mate!"

I bowed in return and entered the grocer's shop.

9

THE TALKATIVE
SHOPKEEPER

OLD SAM STILTON LEANED COMFORTABLY ON THE counter, chatting with a customer. He had trim side whiskers and a round, chubby face.

The customer couldn't have been a very busy mousewife, for they gossiped about everything from taxes to toothbrushes.

Basil motioned me over to the small post-office nook. "We won't disturb them, Dawson. Let's study the WANTED posters, for it's always a pleasure to see familiar faces!"

There wasn't a criminal he failed to recognize. "Look, here's Clarence the Crook. Remember the Anti-Detective League? For months they robbed every detective they caught out alone after dark. Mouseland Yard was baffled, and Inspector Vole called me in on the case.

"Disguising myself, I joined the league and learned that Clarence was the ringleader. I gathered enough evidence to jail the whole gang. But I see from this poster that Clarence is out again. Ssh!"

Mr. Stilton stood before us, peering over his gold-rimmed spectacles. The mousewife had gone.

"Sorry I couldn't get to you sooner, Cap'n. But when Mrs. Boswell's tongue starts waggin'—"

I thought—and *your* tongue, too, you old busybody!

But Basil smiled blandly. "We didn't mind the wait."

"Can I 'elp you? There's many as gets their supplies at Sam Stilton's shop."

Basil wrote out a list. "I'll be wantin' these. We sail for Australia within the week."

The grocer climbed a ladder and began taking tins of food from the shelves. While he did this, Basil chattered away.

"This voyage'll be my last, Mr. Stilton. A house and a garden, that's the ticket when I settle down, and Mousecliffe seems as good a place as any. I'll be needin' a bit of land and someone to build me a house. Know of a good spot?"

Stilton climbed down. "There's some nice 'igh ground just outside town. Good view o' the ocean, too. That's what I'd pick if I was retirin'."

"Aren't you from a big city?" asked Basil. "You can always tell a city mouse from a country mouse."

"That I am, Cap'n. Come from London, I do, but big city bustle ain't for me. Been livin' here a long time. Wouldn't trade this spot for all the cheese in Switzerland."

And then the talkative shopkeeper was off on his favorite subject—Sam Stilton!

He gave us his entire life's history, from babyhood to old age. It seemed as though someone had wound him up, like a mechanical toy, and that the words would never stop coming until the machinery ran down.

I was bored, but Basil nodded in all the proper places, pretending interest in Stilton's story. At last the detective's patience was rewarded.

"Say, Cap'n, didn't you mention needin' somebody to build you an 'ouse?"

"That I did. No hurry—we won't be back for six months, maybe a year."

"Well, there's nobody better fit for the job than 'Arry 'Awkins. Best carpenter in these parts."

"Hawkins, eh?" repeated Basil. "I'll take care to remember that name. Thank you."

Stilton lowered his voice. "Confidentially, Skipper, that mouse 'as been actin' strange lately. His Missus usually does their shoppin'. But for two days now he's been comin' in 'imself, buyin' a lot of extra food. Makes you wonder."

"Wonder about what?" inquired the detective.

"Things like—where's the food goin'? Who's it meant for? Why was a box of sweets stickin'

out of his pocket? Why didn't 'e take the grocer-
ies home, instead of walkin' the other way with
'em? And he looks as scared as someone who
smells cheese but fears a trap. My guess is—'Arry
'Awkins is in trouble! But it would never do for
'is wife to find out—don't tell a soul!"

"Our lips are sealed," promised Basil, as he
paid for his purchases. "It's been a pleasure to
meet you. One of my sailors will pick up the supplies before we ship out."

"Much obliged for your trade, Cap'n Baker.
And I 'opes you'll settle in Mousecliffe-on-Sea."

They shook paws, and we left Sam Stilton's

shop. As we walked along, I could tell that Basil was pleased.

"That chatterbox of a grocer has told me all I needed to know. Angela and Agatha not only love sweets, but have hearty appetites as well. Hawkins is trying to keep them happy."

"Are they aboard the yacht?" I asked.

"No, that would be too risky—the crew might talk. Obviously the Terrible Three have ordered him to hide the twins somewhere and to see that they do not escape. And speaking of Hawkins— here he comes!"

Our disguises were so perfect that he did not recognize us. Basil even bumped into him pur- posely, looking straight at him, and apologized.

"It's all right, Cap'n," mumbled the carpenter, continuing down the street.

Sam Stilton had been right. Hawkins was a dreadfully worried mouse. His eyes darted from side to side as though he were in deadly fear.

Watching him enter the grocer's shop, Basil said, "You may be sure the food and sweets are his own idea. The Terrible Three are not good- hearted."

He halted at the police station. "We'll look up our friend Hawkins later. Now for our final errand of the afternoon."

We entered and disclosed our identities. Police Constable Clewes was quite impressed by Basil.

"Sir, it's an honor to meet so famous a sleuth. I've read about every one of your cases."

They stepped to one side and talked in low tones for several minutes. I was not invited to join them. Then Clewes escorted us to the door.

"You will await my signal," said Basil. "Is everything perfectly clear to you? A mistake in timing could mean failure!"

The constable nodded. "I'm sure your plan will succeed, sir. It's the biggest thing I've ever handled. But before you go, will you give me your autograph? My children would be thrilled. Myself, too, for that matter."

Basil took pen in paw and obliged. The other police crowded around, and he was kept busy scrawling his signature for some time.

As soon as we got outside, he began to massage his paw, complaining, "My writing muscles are cramped."

"Tut, tut, my dear genius," I teased. "Such is the price of fame!"

10

WE STEAL
ABOARD THE YACHT

WHEN WE ARRIVED AT THE INN, I ASKED, "WHAT was the secret plan you and the constable discussed?"

Basil smiled. "Curiosity killed a cat, you know. Tonight will tell the tale!"

For the rest of the afternoon we lounged in our rooms. Basil put on his Angora robe and curled up in a chair for a much-needed catnap.

At five, he awoke and dressed. We descended to the dining room. "Eat hearty," advised my friend. "I don't know when or where we'll be having our next meal."

Promptly at six, he said, none too softly, "The

time is ripe! While the Terrible Three dine at the Flying Squirrel, you and I will board their yacht!"

"Basil, you should have lowered your voice."

He winked. "Do you really think so? Come along!"

We walked to the very end of town and continued on until we came to a lonely, windswept beach.

Behind some rocks was a small dinghy.

"Clewes left it for us," said Basil. "Are you armed?"

I patted the revolver in my back pocket.

"Dawson, we are dealing with dangerous
ruffians. You can still return to the safety of
the inn."

I squared my shoulders. "Stuff and nonsense! We
started this together and we'll finish it together."

His eyes twinkled. "If it doesn't finish us first!"

Far across the water gleamed the lights of the
yacht. We got the dinghy afloat and rowed swiftly
and silently toward the *Victoria*.

An enormous moon hung low in the sky.

I bent to the oars, wondering idly about the truth of the old saying that the moon is made of green cheese.

We could hear the crew singing a rollicking sea chantey. The voices grew louder, and quite suddenly the yacht loomed before us.

A rope ladder hung over the side of the vessel. Unobserved, we climbed up stealthily.

We went belowdecks. After opening the doors of several cabins and peering within, Basil cried, "At last—a typewriter! Let us hope it is the one I am seeking."

He took the kidnappers' letter from his pocket and put a blank sheet of paper in the machine. I watched as he copied the note word for word.

Then he whipped out a pocket lens and compared the two notes. "There is no doubt of it, Dawson—the original was typed on this machine!"

"But isn't all typewriting more or less alike?"

"My dear fellow, that's not so. Typewriting can definitely be identified as the work of a certain machine. We judge it as we judge handwriting. Each typewriter has its own habits, even when it

is in perfect condition, and this one is not. Let us take these two notes, for example."

Interested, I looked over his shoulder.

"Notice the peculiar slant to the letter L," he pointed out. "Also observe that each capital B is minus part of its stem and that every period has punched a hole through the paper. No two typewriters type exactly alike, yet the typing on these two notes is almost identical. Therefore, they are both the work of the same machine."

"Remarkable!" I exclaimed. "Yet it seems so simple when properly explained. You must have put in a great deal of study on the subject."

"True. A detective must be expert in many fields."

Suddenly he pricked up his ears. "Hark!"

I heard swiftly running footfalls from above, coming closer and closer.

Basil crammed both notes into his pocket.

"Remember, Dawson—we have the evidence, but the criminals have not been caught. Now we shall meet them in person, precisely as I planned. Two of their spies were in the dining room of the inn, and I made certain that they overheard where we were going. Here they come—put up a good fight!"

The door swung open, and the Terrible Three came charging in, followed by several husky sailors!

11

CAPTURED BY THE
TERRIBLE THREE!

AT ONCE, BASIL HURLED HIMSELF FORWARD, fighting like a wildcat.

I myself battled with a strength I never dreamed I had, tackling one enemy after another. Then two of them sat on me, and I was powerless to move.

I saw that my muscular friend was being held down by several sailors. He had already knocked three of them senseless.

But we were only two against many, and we were soon disarmed and tightly bound.

The Terrible Three stood over us, scowling.

"Our spies heard you say you were comin' here," said one of them. "You're no ship's Cap'n, and you ain't no first mate. Who *are* you, and why did you sneak aboard?"

"You may not recognize me," declared Basil calmly, "but I can name each one of you—Barney the Bank Robber, Freddie the Forger, and Percy the Pickpocket. Now you've become kidnappers! In the name of our good and gracious Queen—commit no more crimes!"

Freddie the Forger rubbed at Basil's cheek. Some of the greasepaint came off.

"In disguise, eh? Well, shiver my timbers if it ain't our old enemy—Basil, the scientific sleuth! And Doc Dawson, too! What a catch!"

"It's *you* who'll be caught," said Basil sternly. "And you'll pay for your crimes—I'll see to it!"

"Not a chance, you snoop! You'll be too busy playin' tag with the fishes at the bottom of the ocean!"

Percy the Pickpocket laughed harshly. "Thought you'd trap us, eh? Tomorrow our gang goes to Baker Street to chase everybody out. As for the twins, we'll keep 'em ourselves. That'll teach you to stick your nose into our business!"

"Take 'em on deck, crew," ordered Barney

the Bank Robber. "We'll soon be up to heave 'em overboard. It'll be more fun than burglin' the Bank of England!"

We were carried above and dumped on deck. The sailors turned their backs and began singing again.

Basil squirmed close. "Quick, Dawson—the ropes!"

I had visited my dentist recently, and my teeth

were in excellent condition. Bending my head, I gnawed steadily away until Basil was free.

At once he stood up and gave three loud, sharp squeaks.

Dozens of police, led by Constable Clewes, came swarming over the rails of the yacht! It was a bitter battle, but the forces of law and order won.

Clewes tipped his cap to Basil. "I thought you'd never give the signal, sir. Our boats were waiting on the starboard side, ready to carry out your plan."

"Well done!" Basil handed him the kidnap note. "This evidence will put the Terrible Three behind bars. The typewriter is below—take it with you."

The constable paused. "I trust the police will receive some of the credit for the capture."

"Tut, tut, Clewes! *All* the credit will go to you and your brave force. Leave my name out of it!"

Then he beamed most happily at the Terrible Three, whose faces were as black as thunderclouds.

"So your scheme failed, eh? In his poem 'To a Mouse,' Robert Burns, a wise human poet, wrote:

```
The best-laid schemes o' mice an' men
        gang aft agley
```

I often wish that Burns had been a mouse."

He lit his meerwood pipe. "And now, my Not-So-Terrible Three, where are the twins?"

"We'll never squeal!" they shouted hoarsely.

"Then I'll find out for myself. And I wish you all a nice, long vacation in Mousemoor Prison!"

12

HARRY HAWKINS
TALKS

IT WAS WELL PAST MIDNIGHT WHEN A POLICE launch put us ashore.

"Will you need any help, sir?" asked Clewes.

"No, thank you, Constable. I believe we can handle the rest of this matter ourselves."

A chill wind was blowing as we made our way back to town. We passed the inn, and I thought longingly of my comfortable bed.

But Basil did not stop. He strode on so rapidly that I had difficulty in keeping pace.

We went along wide, spacious avenues lined with beautiful homes. Then the wide avenues gave way to narrow, crooked lanes. The houses

69

grew smaller and shabbier, and were crowded close together.

At last Basil halted before a neat but tumble-down dwelling at the end of a grass-grown lane.

The upper windows were dark, but a dim light burned downstairs. Basil crept close and peeped inside.

"We're in luck," he whispered. "There's Hawkins, dozing in his rocker. We dare not ring the bell at this hour. I'll fling some pebbles at the window."

The rattle of the pebbles awoke Hawkins, who rubbed his eyes and looked sleepily about.

"Psst!" Basil tapped lightly on the pane until the carpenter saw him and came to the window.

"What do you want so late at night, Cap'n?"

"You had better step outside," said Basil in a low voice, "unless you wish your wife to know of your connection with the Terrible Three."

The carpenter cringed, and rushed outside. "Who are you, and what do you want of me?"

"Then you don't recognize us, Hawkins. I am Basil of Baker Street, and this is Dr. Dawson."

He stared hard at us. "I'd never 'a' knowed you, sirs. Did you track me down, all the way from London?"

"Never mind about that," replied Basil sternly. "Where have you hidden Angela and Agatha?"

Hawkins was terrified. "I can't tell you."

"They've threatened you, then?"

The carpenter hung his head. "The one thing on earth I'm afeard of is those three. There's no tellin' what they'll do to my family if I talk."

"Then I deduced correctly," remarked Basil. "You were dragged into this against your will."

"I'll tell you as much as I can, Mr. Basil. Me an' mine have always been straight, honest folk. The Terrible Three asked me to do some cabinet-work on their yacht. Jobs were scarce, and not knowin' who they were, I agreed. I had my family to feed. But one day I heard them talk of kidnappin' the twins. I said I'd go to the police, but they just laughed, said I'd never see my own young 'uns again if I went. Scared me half out o' me wits, they did! Then one o' them said, 'Let's make him deliver the note and have him hide the twins instead o' havin' one o' the gang do it. Then he won't run tattlin' to the law.'

"Now I'm in it up to my neck, just as deep as they are. But I had to help them, on account of my family."

"Set your fears at rest," said Basil. "They will menace you no more, for they are in prison."

"Thank heavens!" Hawkins fell to his knees and clutched at the detective's legs. "But does this mean *I'll* go to jail, too? Spare me, I beg of you! Think of my good wife, and my eight young 'uns—such a disgrace would break their hearts!"

"It is precisely they of whom I am thinking. Take us to the twins and I promise that the police will know nothing of what you did. But if the Terrible Three reveal your part in this affair, I'll see to it that you get a light sentence or none at all. The honest life you've led will be in your favor, and so will the fact that you were forced into this."

Tears of gratitude sprang to Hawkins' eyes as Basil helped him to his feet.

"Thank you, sir! The twins are in an old deserted barn in the woods outside Mousecliffe. I'll take you to 'em myself. Nice, sweet children they are. I've tried to be kind to the poor little things."

"I am well aware of that," said Basil. "You bought extra food for them, and sweets."

Hawkins' mouth hung open. "How did you know?"

"No matter. Let us start at once."

"Right, sir. I'll fetch a lantern."

He hurried us through town, taking a short cut, and soon we were entering the woods.

He was in a cheerier frame of mind, now that he had confessed. "It's like a load's been lifted off my shoulders. I'll gladly face my punishment, and then I'll make a new start in life."

The faint gleam of his lantern guided us. It was raining, and our clothes were soaked through.

Even in dry weather, going through such dense forest would have been difficult. The rainfall grew heavier, and often we sank in mud up to our ankles.

Despite these discomforts, I was in high spirits.

In a little while we would find the twins, and this dangerous case would be closed!

13
THE FIGHT IN
THE OLD BARN

HAWKINS STOPPED AT A TREE THAT HAD ONCE been struck by lightning.

"The path to the barn is over yonder." A few steps more and we were out of the woods. With a feeling of thankfulness, I sighted the old deserted barn. It stood on a slight rise of ground, half hidden by masses of overgrown shrubbery, and it had a lonely look.

We plowed through shoulder-high weeds to get there. The door hung crazily from one rusty hinge. It gave way slowly, creaking as though in protest.

Inside, Hawkins held up his lantern, which glimmered feebly in the gloom. It was an eerie place, dusty and long unused. Cobwebs brushed our faces.

"Angela! Agatha!" called Hawkins eagerly.

A ghostly echo was his only reply. We shouted their names loudly, again and again, but back came the same mocking echo.

"They're locked in an upstairs room," said the worried Hawkins, "and usually answer the minute I call. I wonder what's happened."

I, too, wondered. Had the Terrible Three hidden the twins elsewhere, without telling the carpenter?

I moved a few feet away and began to pray silently.

Then Basil laughed. "Do you realize that it's past three in the morning? They must be sound asleep."

I sighed with relief, then stiffened in fear!

There was a whirring of wings around my head, and a giant thing with great golden eyes swooped down upon me!

I heard weird hoots and screeches, and I knew that the worst had come to pass. I was being attacked by our ancient enemy, the barn owl!

"Help! In heaven's name, HELP ME!"

Before the creature could fly away with me, my two friends were upon him.

Their bravery was unbelievable! They climbed up on the great feathered body and rained heavy blows upon the monster with sticks they had picked up. They bit, they scratched, they kicked!

I dangled helplessly in midair, for a sharp claw had hooked itself into my jacket.

Hawkins fought with the strength of ten mice—never for one moment did he stop drumming at the owl with his stick!

The claw loosened, then tightened again as the bird made one last effort to fly off with me.

But Basil and Hawkins were too much for him!

Ever so slowly the claw relaxed its grip. Half-fainting, I slumped to the floor.

The owl must have been badly hurt, for he, too, fell to the floor. He lay there, his body heaving as though in pain.

My friends quickly dragged me a safe distance away.

Hawkins spat out a mouthful of feathers, and leaned against the wall, panting heavily.

Basil cautiously approached our fallen enemy. The golden eyes gleamed angrily, but my friend stared back, unafraid. He began to talk calmly, in the manner of a teacher addressing a class.

"This owl is badly hurt. He will be unable to move for some time. Luckily, the creature is not yet full-grown, or Dawson would have been gobbled up before you could say 'The Owl and the Pussycat'! We would never have won a battle

with an adult owl. This one is nine inches long—
about twice our own size. The average British
barn owl grows to fourteen inches in length. So
much for natural history."

He helped me up. "Can you walk?"

I took a few steps. "I'm still shaky, but it will
pass. I'll never forget this experience. Nor shall I
ever forget that you two heroes saved my life, at
the risk of your own!"

"It was the least I could do," said Hawkins
modestly. "Let's climb the ladder. I can't wait
to see those twins' faces when they get a look at
who's come to fetch 'em home!"

14

THE TWINS
AT LAST!

WE CLIMBED THE LADDER TO THE LOFT.

Hawkins halted before a narrow door. He fitted a long key into the padlock, and the door swung open, revealing a large room.

In the middle of the floor lay a box of half-nibbled chocolates.

Beside it, covered with dirt and grime, and with their pinafores all tattered and torn, lay Angela and Agatha, fast asleep!

They were such a welcome sight that I even enjoyed listening to their delicate snoring.

My silent prayer had been answered—the twins were safe and unharmed!

We shook them gently, and they awoke, staring sleepily about. Basil and I rubbed some of our makeup off, and they recognized us.

Shouting with delight, they leaped upon us and smeared our cheeks with wet, sticky kisses.

After a while Basil waved them away. "Little mouselings, your parents will soon shower you with affection. As for myself, I'd sooner tackle a tabbycat than put up with all this kissing!"

The twins giggled, and hugged Hawkins instead.

Basil looked at them sternly. "All this trouble

and worry could have been avoided if you children hadn't gone off with a stranger."

Angela hung her head. "We'll never do it again!"

And Agatha added solemnly, "Cross our hearts!"

Outside, the black of night had given way to the pink dawn. Tired but happy, we made our way back to the Greymouse Inn.

There I got out my little black bag and gave the twins a complete checkup. I was glad to find that they were in perfect health.

Hawkins offered to bathe them. "I'm quite used to it, sirs, with eight of me own."

Meanwhile, Basil and I changed into our regular clothes. It was good to be our own selves again.

When the shops opened, we sent Hawkins out to buy new pinafores for the twins.

Freshly scrubbed and shiny clean, they were two of the prettiest little white mice in all England!

Basil attracted many stares in the lobby. Now that he was no longer in disguise, everyone recognized the Sherlock Holmes of the Mouse World.

After breakfast, Hawkins guided us to Working-ton Station. A train was about to leave for London, and we slipped into an empty compartment.

Basil leaned out. "Hawkins, we Baker Street mice plan a school annex and other buildings. We should be happy to hire a fine carpenter like yourself and to provide lodgings for your family in Holmestead. If you should serve a prison term, the job will wait."

The train began moving slowly out of the station.

Harry Hawkins ran alongside, waving and call-ing, "Bless you, Basil—and bless all of you!"

15

BACK TO
BAKER STREET

THE TWINS ENJOYED WATCHING THE TREES AND houses flash by and glued their noses to the window all the way to London.

At Euston Station, we overheard a lady directing her driver to Baker Street. We helped Angela and Agatha up, and all four of us perched on the rear of the hansom cab.

What a heartwarming scene took place when we reached the cellar of Baker Street, Number 221B!

As Basil remarked later, watching the reunion of mother and children was ample reward for all the dangers we had faced.

The twins scampered on ahead, calling, "Mummy! Papa! We're home!"

There was a look of heavenly joy on Mrs. Proudfoot's face as she clasped Angela and Agatha in her arms.

"My darlings! My very own darlings!"

Mr. Proudfoot wiped away his happy tears, and my own eyes were far from dry.

Many friends and neighbors crowded around to congratulate Basil.

When we returned to our rooms, Mrs. Judson

bustled in with a cheese soufflé, Basil's favorite dish.

She beamed proudly at him. "Sir, you are the world's greatest detective!"

"The second greatest, Mrs. Judson. Mr. Sherlock Holmes, of course, ranks first."

Afterward, we settled in comfortable chairs before the fire.

I looked searchingly at Basil. He had been working at a mad pace and seemed unusually tired.

"As your doctor, I prescribe a full week's rest."

Basil slouched down in his chair and yawned.

"Sounds fearfully dull, Dawson."

It was a wild, windy night, with a blizzard raging.

Suddenly our doorbell clanged. Basil sat bolt upright, no longer bored.

Our mousekeeper rapped on the door. "A caller for you, Basil. Says it's a matter of life or death."

He turned to me pleadingly. "My dear doctor, can't that week's rest wait? Only a most exciting case would bring a mouse out on a night like this!"

I shrugged my shoulders. "I suppose you'd

grumble and groan for days if I denied you. Get on with it!"

The famous sleuth faced the door, his weariness magically gone, his eyes agleam with eagerness.

"Mrs. Judson, I am ready to receive my caller."

Read more about Basil,
the mouse detective, in . . .

Basil and the Cave of Cats

Previously titled *Basil and the Pygmy Cats*

THE CLUE OF THE GOLDEN GOBLET

MINIATURE CATS! BREATHES THERE, IN ALL THE WORLD,
A mouse who is not stirred by those two words?

Did the miniature monsters actually exist? Our
leading mouse scientists were not certain, but they
all believed the answer would be found in the Orient.

It was Basil of Baker Street, the Sherlock
Holmes of the Mouse World, who solved the
mystery. He used his skill as a scientific sleuth
to bring to light secrets long hidden behind the
curtains of the past, secrets no other mouse had
been able to discover.

Professor Ratigan, leader of the mouse under-
world, stalked him at every turn! Danger was

Basil's constant companion. Ratigan's spies were at the border, in the jungle, on the ship, and—

But let me tell you how the adventure began. . . .

The year is 1894. The place is London, England, at Baker Street, Number 221B, where live Mr. Sherlock Holmes and his friend, Dr. John H. Watson.

Mr. Holmes is the World's Greatest Human Detective. Basil is the World's Greatest Mouse Detective, and I, Dr. David Q. Dawson, am his friend.

We dwell in the cellar of 221B, in the mouse town of Holmestead, which Basil named after his hero. My friend would often scurry up secret passageways to Mr. Holmes' rooms. There he would take notes in shortpaw as the human detective told Dr. Watson exactly how he solved his difficult cases. One might say that Basil studied at the great man's feet.

Did Mr. Holmes ever see his small admirer, hidden in a corner? I believe he did, and that it pleased him to pass his methods on to a mouse.

And *such* a mouse! I am of average height, about five inches tall, but Basil towers a full inch above me.

My notebook is crammed with accounts of his cases. I am a busy doctor, but whenever possible, I take pen in paw to write of his achievements. Would that I had time to narrate them all!

There was the Mystery of the Bald-Headed Mouse, a bank director. One foggy morning he stepped out of his office and vanished, along with a lot of the bank's money. Mouseland Yard detectives sought him with no success, but Basil studied the clues and found the bald banker in Edinburgh, wearing a wig and using another name. Most of the stolen funds were untouched, for spending large sums in Scotland would have drawn attention to the thief at once.

Then there was the Case of the Guinea-Pig Gang. The honest mice of London dared not venture out at night until Basil cleverly found the criminals' hideout and had them all jailed.

But of all his cases, Basil's own favorite is the Adventure of the Cave of Cats. It put to use all his remarkable skill as a sleuth, plus his vast knowledge of the science of archeology.

Basil's hobby was archeology. He had discovered Rockhenge, the ancient mouse ruins near London.

Interviewed by newspapermice, Basil said, "The most exciting detective work in the world is archeology! As we dig, clues keep turning up. Arrowheads, old weapons, broken bowls—any or all may hold clues to the life and times of prehistoric mice. The calendar stone I found at Rockhenge, for example, proved that mice perfected a 365-day calendar long before mankind. Clearly, archeology is the highest form of detective work, for lessons we learn from the past help mice to build a better, brighter future!"

The clues concerning the cave of cats were to take us halfway across the world, to the Far East.

Originally we had planned our trip to the Orient for a different reason—to restore the Maharajah of Bengistan to his rightful throne.

Cyril the Stoolpigeon had brought word that our enemy, Professor Ratigan, now ruled Bengistan, a mouse kingdom near India.

Too large to enter, the pigeon stood at our window to tell us what a little bird had told him.

In a surprise move the Professor and his gang had stormed and taken the palace. They guarded the border day and night. The Maharajah was unharmed, but kept prisoner in his private apartments in the palace. Ratigan taxed everything, even cheese! Mice too poor to pay the tax starved. And all the tax money went into Ratigan's pockets!

"Thank you, Cyril," said Basil. "You may pick up your reward at the back window. Mrs. Judson, our mousekeeper, baked blackberry tarts today."

Cyril, grinning happily, was off in a trice.

Basil's eyes blazed. "That rat Ratigan! Robbing our friend of his throne! I cannot stand idly by— we leave for the Orient at dawn. Can you arrange to have another doctor attend your patients?"

I could, and did, by nightfall. Then, having packed, we relaxed in easy chairs before the fire.

The doorbell jangled, and Mrs. Judson ushered in Dr. Edvard Hagerup, a Norwegian scientist from the British Mousmopolitan Museum.

After we all shook paws, he held up a golden goblet of ancient design. I reproduce it below.

Basil studied the goblet, and chuckled. "My

word! Elotana, Goddess of Goodness! European
mice worshipped her thousands of years ago.
Look—kneeling before her are cats scarcely the
size of mice! Where was the goblet found?"

"In Turkey," said Hagerup. "It proves that
miniature cats existed. We of the Mousmopolitan
know you are going to the Orient. We feel you
are the only mouse who can solve this mystery.
Will you try?"

Basil nodded. "Gladly, after I've captured

Ratigan. A noted archeologist once said, 'One pits one's wits against the past!' How true! This will be the most challenging case of my career!"

Quickly Basil sketched the scene on the goblet, and the Norwegian departed with the original.

That night scores of miniature cats marched through my slumbers, shaking with fright at the sight of me. Seldom have I enjoyed more delightful dreams!

Mermaid Tales

Exciting under-the-sea adventures with
Shelly and her mermaid friends!

Trouble at Trident Academy • Battle of the Best Friends • A Whale of a Tale

Danger in the Deep Blue Sea • The Lost Princess • The Secret Sea Horse • Dream of the Blue Turtle

Treasure in Trident City • A Royal Tea • Tale of Two Sisters • The Polar Bear Express

Wish upon a Starfish • The Circus Under the Sea • Twist and Shout

MermaidTalesBooks.com

Candy Fairies

Chocolate Dreams

Rainbow Swirl

Caramel Moon

Cool Mint

Magic Hearts

Gooey Goblins

The Sugar Ball

A Valentine's Surprise

Bubble Gum Rescue

Double Dip

Jelly Bean Jumble

The Chocolate Rose

A Royal Wedding

Marshmallow Mystery

Frozen Treats

The Sugar Cup

Sweet Secrets

Taffy Trouble

The Coconut Clue

Rock Candy Treasure

A Minty Mess

Visit candyfairies.com for games, recipes, and more!

Nancy Drew

* CLUE BOOK *

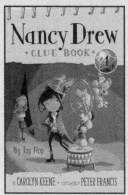

Did you LOVE reading this book?

Visit the Whyville...

Where you can:

○ Discover great books!

○ Meet new friends!

○ Read exclusive sneak peeks and more!

Log on to visit now!
bookhive.whyville.net